THE BOOLA PAN

THE BOOLA PAN
and
Other Benjy Stories

Helen C. Noordewier

BAKER BOOK HOUSE
Grand Rapids, Michigan

For all the children at Sylvan School
who have walked and talked with me
and especially Eddie.

Contents

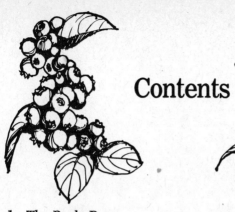

THE BOOLA PAN
and Other Benjy Stories

1 The Boola Pan

Benjy looked up from his bowl of cereal. Suddenly he remembered. "Mama!" he shouted. "You have to choose a present! Tomorrow is your birthday!"

"Yes, I know," Mama said, and she smiled.

Papa put his spoon on the table. He looked closely at Mama because he felt that she had already chosen the present she wanted and he hoped that it would not cost too much.

Five-year-old Fritzie across the table was hoping, too. He wished that Mama would choose a puppy. He thought she might, because he had once asked for a puppy and Mama had said, "No, Fritzie. Puppies are for mothers. Mothers end up doing all the work for a puppy."

Benjy didn't know what he hoped Mama would choose, but he was anxious. "Couldn't you tell us today?" he asked.

"No, no," Mama said. "It is not wise to tell before the birthday."

The next morning was dark and rainy, but Mama's face was bright and smiling. She was ready to choose! The children could tell!

"What is it? What is it?" they shouted.

"Sit down," Mama said. Then, in a very soft voice, she told them. "I would like one row of blueberry bushes in the front yard, just this side of the road and straight across from the driveway to the fence."

The children looked disappointed. So did Papa.

"Blueberry bushes!" he shouted. "Blueberry bushes! The whole back acre is full of blueberry bushes!"

"That is the trouble," Mama said. "Because they are in the back I cannot go there to pick. Baby Lisha sleeps too much of the time. And besides, they are for selling. In the front yard they would be all mine. Mine for blueberry pies and blueberry muffins and blueberry pancakes."

Benjy and Fritzie licked their lips, but Papa said, "They will look ugly in the front yard."

"Oh, no, they will look very beautiful," Mama said. "In the summer they will be rich. Rich with purple berries and dark green leaves. And in the fall they will be scarlet. They will be like a fence of fire across the whole front yard."

"They will be dirt-catchers," Papa said. "All the litter from the road will blow into them."

"That is true," Mama said, "but Benjy and Fritzie have good, strong hands and I will buy them each a pair of gloves. Work gloves just like Papa wears, only made for little hands."

Mama almost always got her way and it was not long before the bushes were planted. They were quite small at first, but just as Mama said, they were "rich and green in the summer and scarlet in the fall."

It was exciting when the bushes began to bear

10

fruit. Picking the berries was fun, and Mama thought up wonderful desserts for all of them.

Soon, however, funny things began to happen that Mama was not at all ready for. The trouble was other people. Just because the bushes were close to the road, people in cars thought they belonged to anyone who wanted to stop and pick the berries.

Mama was upset. What could she do?

"Benjy," she said. "Can you help me? What shall we do about the people?"

"Scare them away," Benjy said.

"And how shall we do that?" Mama asked.

"Do like I do when I scare chickens out of the garden," Benjy answered. "Grab that little old pan that hangs on the kitchen wall. Run outdoors and bang it hard. Maybe it will scare the people away too."

Mama thought about it and when the next car full of people stopped she took the little pan, banged it hard with her hand and running toward the bushes she shouted, "Boola! Boola! Boola!"

The people quickly got back into their car and drove away.

"See," Benjy said. "It scares chickens and it scares people too. But why did you say boola, boola, boola?"

"I don't know," Mama said. "It just happened. I did not even stop to think it up. Do you think it's a scary word?"

"Yes," said Benjy. "It's a scary word."

"But listen," Mama said. "I do not have time to do all the chasing. You are a big boy. You must help me with the people as well as with the chickens. When people come you must grab the

11

boola pan."

That was something Benjy had not thought about and it was something Benjy did not like to do. But Fritzie was too small and Papa was always out on the farm, so the chasing belonged to Mama and to Benjy.

And then it happened. One day, as Benjy and Fritzie were watching, Mama was shouting, "Boola, boola, boola," and a whole family scampered back into their car. But as they drove away a little boy called from the back seat, "You are a witch! You are a mean, old witch!"

Benjy and Fritzie looked at Mama.

"Are you a witch?" Fritzie asked.

"I am not a witch," Mama said.

"The boy said so," Fritzie answered. "And when you run out with the boola pan and your hair is flying behind you, you look like a witch."

"I am not a witch," Mama said again, but now she was troubled. This was not good. Sometimes she did feel like a mean, old witch, always chasing people. Was this what the blueberry bushes were doing to her? They were her very own bushes, she knew, and they did not belong to the people. But a witch! She did not want to be a witch! What could she do? She thought about it all day and far into the night, long after everyone else in the family was asleep, but it did not help. Mama had a problem and she just could not think how to solve it.

Saturday came and Benjy and Fritzie did not have to go to school. They were busy playing in the front yard when a little boy about Benjy's age peeked around the corner of the blueberry bushes.

"Hi," he said.

The boys looked up.

"Hi," they both said.

"What's your name?" the boy asked.

"I'm Benjy and he's Fritzie," Benjy said. "What's your name?"

"Joshua," he said. "I live by the river. What are those?" he asked, pointing to the bushes.

"Blueberries," said Benjy.

"Are they good to eat?" Joshua asked.

"They're good," Benjy said.

"Are they sour?"

"No, they're sweet," Benjy said. "Here, try some," and he picked three and laid them in Joshua's hand.

"M-m-m-m," Joshua said. "I like 'em. Could we have some more? Maybe we could have a blueberry party."

Fritzie and Benjy loved a party, and Benjy had an idea.

"Wait a minute," he said. "I'll be right back."

Quickly he ran into the house and took the little boola pan from its usual place. Holding it high he shouted, "It's not for scaring. It's for holding the blueberries."

The children picked until the pan was full and then they sat down by the fence to share the berries.

Before very long Mama came outdoors.

"Fritzie, Benjy," she called. "Where are you?"

"Way over here by the fence," Fritzie called back.

"What are you doing by the fence?" Mama called. And then she saw there were three children, so she walked over to them.

"What are you doing?" she asked again.

And then Mama saw the berries.

"What!" she said. "Berries in the boola pan!"

"Yes," said Benjy. "We have a friend."

"So I see," said Mama. "It's nice to have a friend."

"He's Joshua," said Benjy, "and he likes blueberries."

"I see that, too," Mama said. "Did you wash the berries?"

"Yes, at the pump," Fritzie answered.

"Why don't you bring them in the kitchen?" Mama said. "Maybe Joshua would like them with brown sugar and cream."

Joshua did like them. So did Benjy and Fritzie. And when the blueberry party was over the three boys found lots of things to amuse themselves. The morning passed much too swiftly, and when Joshua left Benjy came running to Mama.

"He's coming again tomorrow," he said excitedly. "He's a good friend."

Mama was happy. She knew it was far better for the boys to have a friend than always to play by themselves.

That evening, after the boys were in bed, Mama finished the dishes. The last thing she washed was the boola pan, and as she hung it on the nail, she gave it a little pat and said, "Little pan, today you helped to make a friend." And Joshua, she was sure, did not think she was a witch.

After she went to bed, Mama thought over all the happenings of the day. She thought about Papa and Lisha and the boys and Joshua and the boola pan. Suddenly everything was clear to her. She knew what to do about the blueberries!

14

She knew what to do about the boola pan! And with a happy heart, Mama fell asleep.

The next morning was quiet at the breakfast table. When all had finished their food, Mama stood up.

"I have something to say," she said.

"And what is it?" Papa asked. He knew it must be something special.

Mama walked to the wall where the boola pan hung. She took it from the special nail, and holding it high in the air, she announced, "There will be no more chasing with the boola pan."

Everyone was surprised. Papa looked at her questioningly.

"How will you keep the berries for ourselves?" he asked.

"We will not keep the berries for ourselves," Mama said. "Yesterday this little pan helped to make a friend for Fritzie and Benjy. Perhaps it can do the same for all of us. We will let the people pick the berries, enough to fill the boola pan, and what is left we will use for ourselves." She looked at Papa, and there was a little twinkle in her eyes.

"Maybe," she said, "if the people take too many, Papa can spare a few from the back acre."

"That I can," Papa said.

And so the boola pan found a new home. Papa hung it on the old pump, along with a big sign that said, "Dear Friends. You may have as many blueberries as the boola pan will hold. One pan, full, will make a big blueberry pie."

Oh, yes, the people came and the people picked. Mama always found out who they were and where they lived and told them to come again. They called her the pie lady.

But when they got back into their cars, they all wondered about the same things.

"Why are those people so nice?" they all said. "And why do they call that pan a boola pan?"

That is something they never found out, but it is something I know and something you know too.

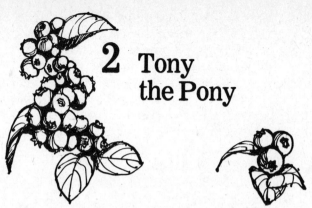

2 Tony the Pony

"Benjy, did you take care of the goat?"

It was the same question that Papa asked every night, and tonight Papa got the same answer that he always did.

"Yes, Papa, I took care of the goat. Every night I take care of the goat because I love him very much. He is safe in the barn and the goat wagon stands beside him."

"Good," Papa said. "And now to bed, Benjy. Tomorrow we go to the market, you know, and that will be a long day."

Benjy said goodnight and crawled into his bed close beside his little brother, Fritzie. He thought about tomorrow and all of the things he would see and do in the market place. Papa had long ago taught him how to make change for the customers and he fell asleep figuring how much change he would give for a dollar when the carrots cost fifty-five cents.

The next day began bright and clear, except for pink clouds where the sun was playing peek-a-boo with the morning.

"Take your sweater," Mama said. "Autumn days

can be cold. The lunch is on the front seat of the truck. And be a good helper for Papa today."

Benjy promised he would, and said goodbye to Fritzie and Mama. Papa had the truck loaded. There were green beans and lima beans, several different kinds of squash, carrots, beets and potatoes, apples, pears, and a few pumpkins. With Papa and Benjy in the front seat with the lunch, it made a very full truck.

Papa's stall in the market place was in the middle, which Papa liked and Benjy liked. If you were too far on either end the people did not want to come to you. In the middle everyone walked past and the buying was better. But there was more to the market than fruits and vegetables. There was the popcorn stand and the section for baked goods. At another corner people brought plants to sell, and still another was reserved for homemade articles. There were knitted mittens and pot holders and dolls dressed in many different costumes. There was homemade furniture, and way down at the southern end there were animals for sale—kittens and puppies, rabbits and hamsters, and sometimes little piglets, a few ponies, and a mule or two. Oh, the market was a wonderful place!

Taking everything out of the truck was hard work and Benjy said so.

"Never mind," Papa said. "Little hands are for little things, so you take the little ones and I will take the big ones. But remember, we do not just dump things on the tables. We make it look pretty. Carrots and beets go in big bouquets. People buy more easily when things look pretty."

And so the market day passed swiftly by. Benjy

counted the change carefully, but he noticed that Papa was often watching over his shoulder to make sure Benjy was neither cheating nor over-paying the customers.

The crowds had finally finished their buying and there were only a few stragglers left. This was the time of day Benjy liked best. He could leave the cleanup for Papa and he was free to roam for a little while. He could go to the popcorn stand to buy "just one thing," as Papa said.

Benjy roamed and before he knew it his feet took him to the part of the market where the animals were. He petted the rabbits, counted the piglets, and watched the hamsters. And then there were the ponies. They were not so young and beautiful, but they were still good for a child to ride. Benjy liked the dark brown one the best and soon found out that he liked to be petted. Benjy stroked his long mane and the pony touched Benjy's ear with his nose. And that settled it for Benjy. He liked the pony and the pony liked him. Benjy put his head close beside the pony's head.

"What do you call him?" he asked the owner.

"Why, that's Tony," the farmer said.

"Is he for sale?" Benjy asked.

"Oh, he's for sale all right," the farmer answered. "But it's time for the market to close so he will go back to the farm with me."

"How much does he cost?" Benjy asked.

"Only fifty dollars," said the farmer. "My barn is getting too small for all I have, and he takes a lot of room."

Fifty dollars! That was more money than Benjy could think of, but oh, how he wanted that pony.

In the meantime, Papa was wondering why Benjy did not come back. He sat in the empty truck and waited. He waited a long time and still Benjy did not come.

"Hmph," he said to himself. "Where is that boy? I'd better go and look for him."

But Benjy was not at the popcorn stand. That was already closed. So Papa walked the length of the market. And from a distance he could see him. His face was pressed against the horse's mane.

"Benjy! Benjy!" Papa called, but Benjy did not hear. In his mind he was counting dollars — fifty of them.

"Benjy," Papa called again and came closer. And suddenly, there was Papa standing in front of Benjy and looking a little bit angry.

"I could not find you, son," he said. "I have been all over. And where do I find you? In the animal stall. And what are you doing? Kissing a horse!"

Benjy's face reddened a little.

"He nuzzles me, Papa, so I nuzzle him back," he said. "He's a pony, Papa, and his name is Tony and he's for sale and I would like him to be mine."

"And how much does he cost?" Papa asked.

"Dollars," said Benjy.

"Dollars!" said Papa. "How many dollars?"

"Fifty, Papa."

"Do you have fifty dollars?"

"No, Papa," Benjy said. "Does Papa have fifty dollars?"

"Papa does not!" Papa said. "Not for a pony. What would Mama say if I came home from the market with a horse instead of dollars?"

"Could I earn the dollars, Papa?"

20

"That will be up to you, my boy. Fifty dollars is a lot of money and you will have to plan how to earn it. But you have three good things: quick hands, fast and willing feet, and a good brain. It will take all three to earn your fifty dollars. But you must figure out how to do it."

When Benjy went to bed that night he thought about the market and he thought about Tony when suddenly he remembered. "The goat!" he said. He had forgotten to take care of the goat! The poor little thing was still in the pasture!

Quickly he hopped out of bed, dressed himself, and fairly flew down the stairs.

"Wait a minute. Wait a minute," Mama said. "Why are you out of bed?"

"The goat," said Benjy. "I forgot to take care of the goat."

"Tony the pony is walking in your head too much," Papa said.

But forgetting the goat was a lucky thing for Benjy. As he brought him from the field and put him in the barn beside the goat wagon he suddenly threw his arms around him and hugged him closely.

"Little One," he said. "You are the one who will help me. You will help me to make money. Money to buy a pony named Tony."

Benjy said nothing to Papa about his money scheme, and Papa said nothing more about the pony. Saturday was market day and Benjy waited until then.

When Papa brought the truck out beside the mounds of freshly picked vegetables, Benjy stood ready with the goat and the wagon.

"Little One goes to the market today," Benjy said.

"What!" said Papa. "You are going to sell the goat and also the wagon I made you?"

"No! Oh, no, Papa. Little One will work today. He will give rides around the fence that surrounds the market place. Rides for all the children who come with their mothers. Rides for a quarter. You know, Papa, you said that I must figure out how to make the money for Tony."

Papa smiled a little and wrinkled his brow. "How in the world," he said, "will all the vegetables fit in the truck when it is already carrying a goat and a wagon?"

"The vegetables will go around the goat and the wagon and on the seat," Benjy said. "And I will sit in the wagon. I will make myself very small so that there will be room for potatoes all around me."

Papa laughed. "What a funny looking load I will have today," he said. "But remember, Benjy, the goat must work only a part of the day or he will be too tired. And the rest of the time I will need you to help me."

Giving the rides was fun for Benjy. He felt very important. With one child in the cart, or two if they were very small, Benjy led Little One by his halter around the long fence. Each quarter he put into the small cloth bag tied to his belt that Mama had made for his marbles. The quarters jingled when he walked and he felt very proud. By noon the bag was full—so full that the quarters did not jingle any more. And Benjy knew it was enough for the little goat. He must not get too tired, and so he tied Little One to the fence on a long rope and took the wagon to Papa beside the truck.

"Look, Papa," he said, as he patted the bag full of quarters. His face was all smiles.

Papa shook his head. "Benjy, Benjy," he said. "You are a little money man! A real little money man!"

When they got home, Benjy had something special to show to Mama. He shook the quarters quietly out of the little bag and arranged them in a long, long line on the kitchen floor.

"Mama," he called. "Come and look, Mama!"

Mama's mouth flew open. "What now?" she said.

"A mile of quarters from the goat," Benjy said. "Papa calls me a little money man."

"That you are," said Mama. "And I am very proud of you. But quarters are not dollars, Benjy. You will need dollars."

"But quarters make dollars," Benjy said. "See what a good start I have! Now I will count them."

Touching each quarter with his finger he began. "One, two, three, four, five," he counted, all the way to twenty-seven.

"I have twenty-seven quarters, Mama. Then how many dollars do I have?"

"Figure it out like you do in school," Mama said. "There are twenty-five pennies in a quarter, so it would be twenty-five times twenty-seven. How much would that be?"

Benjy figured a long time. Finally he said, "I did it over and over, Mama, and it's seven hundred and seventy-five."

"That means your quarters are worth seven hundred and seventy-five pennies, or seven dollars and seventy-five cents. But come now, little money man. Clear the floor and put your quarters away. Supper is ready."

Fritzie's eyes shone when Benjy told him about the goat rides. Benjy talked about how some little children were afraid at first and how others begged for another quarter to go around the fence once more. Fritzie wished he was as old as Benjy.

The next Saturday was market day again, but it rained.

"There will be no rides today," Papa said.

Benjy was disappointed but he knew there was no way he could give rides in the rain. He would have to keep busy helping Papa. Carefully he took the precious quarters out of the bag and hid them in his drawer. The empty bag he tied to his belt, just in case he needed it.

It was slow at the market even though there were coverings to keep out the rain. People were not in such a hurry today. There was time to talk.

"Please, mother," a little girl begged as she stood in front of Papa's stall. "Please, may I have that big pumpkin?"

"No, not today," her mother said. "Your daddy is away from home and I have never carved a pumpkin."

"I have carved a pumpkin," Benjy said. "I will carve it for you. For fifty cents I will carve it."

The little girl jumped up and down, clapping her hands.

"Please, mother! Please, mother!" she said.

"All right," the mother said. Turning to Benjy she asked, "How long will it take?"

"I will do it right away," he said.

But Papa said, "You did not ask me, Benjy. Do you have a knife?"

"No, Papa," Benjy said. "But the knife you use to cut off the carrot tops and the beet tops is very sharp. And remember, Papa, you said I had to figure out how to earn the money for Tony all by myself."

"All right," Papa said. "We will try just one."

Benjy went to work. With Papa's felt pen he drew the face on the pumpkin. He made big, round eyes, a triangle nose and a big laughing mouth. Cutting the pumpkin was not easy, but Benjy had done it before so he knew very well how to go about it. Keeping the eyes round was the hardest part, but he managed. Papa watched carefully, smiling now and then to see Benjy work so hard and so carefully. And in a short time the happy little pumpkin face was finished.

The little girl was delighted, and Benjy collected his pay—*two* fifty cent pieces, shiny and new. He put them both in his little cloth bag.

"Wait a minute," Papa said. "Who grew that pumpkin?"

"God sent the sun and the rain, Papa," Benjy said.

"And who planted the seed?" Papa asked.

"You did, Papa," Benjy answered.

"So who gets one of those fifty cent pieces?"

"You do, Papa," Benjy said, and he gave Papa his fair share.

At the end of the day Benjy was only fifty cents richer than he had been in the morning, but he was not sad. He knew what he was going to do. All next week, every day after school he would carve pumpkins. They would be ready for sale on Saturday.

What a beautiful pile of round faces he had. And how very loaded the truck was on Saturday morning. Benjy was back in the goat wagon with his arm around Little One to hold her steady. And packed around them were the pumpkins and the potatoes and the squash and apples that Papa still had to sell.

Mama had made Benjy another little cloth bag, so now there were two tied to his belt. The new one was much larger than the other.

With the rides finished and the pumpkins all sold, the end of the day found both of Benjy's bags very full. Papa was pleased and so was Benjy.

Before they left the market Benjy asked Papa, "May I go to the animals and see if Tony came to the market today?"

That was fine with Papa. "But don't stay too long," he said.

Benjy left on flying feet. But Tony was not there. For a minute his heart sank, but the owner, Mr. Mikita, was there.

"Did you sell Tony?" Benjy asked.

"No, I have rabbits to sell today," Mr. Mikita said. "Tony is home in the field today."

"I am going to buy him when I have enough money," Benjy said.

"That's fine," Mr. Mikita said. "I'll keep him for you. By the way, do you have any friends?"

"Oh, yes, lots of friends at school," Benjy said.

"Why don't you buy a rabbit from me? I have one who will have baby rabbits before very long, I think, and you could sell them to your friends. That will give you more money and it will help me to sell Tony a little sooner."

"I will take the rabbit," Benjy said, and he took two fifty cent pieces from his bag.

"Oh, oh," Papa said when he saw Benjy walking back. "The money man has another idea. Are you going to sell rabbits next?"

"Baby rabbits, Papa, to my friends, and Mr.

Mikita will keep Tony for me. Mr. Mikita lives on the farm next to the schoolhouse."

For the hundredth time, when Benjy came home, the money was shaken out of the sack and counted. He was getting close to his goal now. He had forty-eight dollars and fifty cents. And that was a lot of money.

During the next few days, Papa was doing a lot of thinking and his hands were very busy. Finally he was finished.

"The job is all done," he said to Mama one day.

"What is all done?" Mama asked.

"A stall for Tony," Papa answered.

"Are you going to get the pony soon?" Mama asked.

"Tomorrow," said Papa. "Tomorrow, when Benjy is in school. Mr. Mikita will bring him. It will be a surprise."

"But he will soon have rabbits to sell and he still does not have quite enough money."

"It will do," Papa said. "He has worked hard and I will add the rest. The rabbit money we will save to buy food for the pony."

When Benjy came home from school the next day, he did not know that the new stall in the barn had an occupant. Mama could not help but smile when Benjy came in the door. Papa tried to look very sober.

"Go upstairs and change your clothes, Benjy," Mama said. "There will be a cookie when you are ready."

Benjy did as he was told. And then, quite suddenly, Mama and Papa heard him crying. He came running down the stairs.

"My money, my money," he cried. "My money is gone!"

"Now, now," Mama said. "Dry your tears. Your money is in the barn."

"In the *barn*!" Benjy said. "Why is it in the barn? It is not safe there."

"Oh, I think it is very safe," Papa said. "Come, I will show you."

They all went together, Papa, Mama, Fritzie, and even baby Lisha.

The barn was quite dark, but Papa said, "Look, Benjy! Look over there in the corner."

Benjy looked and Benjy saw.

"Tony," he cried, and he ran and threw his arms around the pony, kissing his mane over and over while tears of happiness trickled down his face.

"Oh, thank you, Papa! Thank you, Mama!" he said again and again.

"Look up," Papa said. "See what the nameplate over the stall says."

Benjy stepped back and read what Papa had painted on a big, beautiful board. It said:

TONY the PONY

presented
to Benjy
by himself

3 Caught with Sugar

"Benjy is not home from school and it is past time, Mama," Fritzie said. "He is always home when the little hand is on the four and the big hand is on the six. But the big hand is already on nine."

Mama looked at the clock. "You are right," she said. "I hope the teacher did not have to keep him after school. But maybe he was a naughty boy today."

Fifteen minutes later Benjy came in. Angrily he put his lunch pail on the floor.

"You are very late," Mama said.

"I know," was all Benjy answered.

"But that does not say anything. 'I know' does not tell me *why*," Mama said.

Benjy looked up and Mama saw the reason why.

"Oh, my," she said. "You have a black eye. You have a shiner."

"It was Carl," Benjy said.

"But it was not only Carl," Mama said. "One boy cannot fight alone. It takes two boys to make a fight."

29

"But he hit me first," Benjy said. "And so I hit him back."

"Does he have a shiner too?" Mama asked.

"Yes, a big one," Benjy said. "I hit him hard."

"I would like to know one thing," Mama said. "What did you do or say to make Carl hit you first?"

"Nothing. Nothing, Mama. He just says he doesn't like me."

"He doesn't like you, Benjy? I always thought you were his friend and playmate! And now he doesn't like you? Why?"

"He told the teacher after school that he just doesn't like me. And when she asked him why, he said he didn't know."

"And then what did the teacher say?" asked Mama.

"She said it was a poor reason for a fight and if people didn't like other people they should surely know the reason why."

"Well," Mama said, "the black eye will soon heal, and we hope tomorrow will be a better day. We will try to catch Carl with sugar."

"With sugar? How can we do that, Mama?" Benjy asked.

"Oh, you will see," Mama said. "If we put salt at one end of the table and sugar at the other end, where do you think the flies will go?"

"To the sugar side, Mama," Benjy said. "Flies like things that are sweet."

"So do people," Mama said. "And I will do a little thinking about a sweet thing."

The next morning Benjy's lunch bucket was heavier than usual.

"What is in the lunch pail today?" he asked.

"Almost the same as usual," Mama said. "But something extra is in there. Two doughnuts, home-made, for recess—one for you, Benjy, and one for Carl. The doughnut will be our sugar, Benjy."

Benjy smiled. He was no longer angry with Carl, and he was sure today would be a better day.

At recess Carl took the doughnut grudgingly. He ate it very fast and then turned to Benjy and said, "But you still ride an old nag."

Benjy felt angry, but he remembered what his mother had said, that it takes two to make a fight.

Mama was waiting when Benjy got home. She was a little anxious.

"How did it go with Carl today?" she asked.

"He ate the doughnut," Benjy said, "but he says I ride an old nag. Tony is not an old nag, is he Mama?"

"No. He is no longer a colt, but neither is he old. He has some good riding years left. But don't think about it. I am glad you don't have another shiner. And now, Benjy, since Tony needs a little exercise, will you ride him to the country store? I would like just a few things."

"That will be a good ride for Tony," Benjy said. "What do you need?"

"Three things," Mama said. "Butter, bread, and peanut butter. Do you want me to make a list for you?"

"Oh, no, Mama," Benjy said. "I can remember. The butter goes on the bread and the peanut butter goes on the butter. That's easy."

Benjy gave Tony a good run and when they reached the store he tied him to the fence. Benjy liked the inside of the store. There was a little bit of everything. He looked at the big case that was full of penny candy, but Benjy had no pennies. There was a big barrel full of dill pickles that smelled sour, but good. They cost ten cents apiece, but Benjy had no money for that, either. There was a baseball glove that looked very good to him and he spent several minutes pushing a toy truck down the counter.

"Can I help you, young man?" the grocer asked.

"Yes, sir," said Benjy. "I need a loaf of bread, butter to put on the bread, and peanut butter to put on top of the butter."

The grocer smiled and gathered the order.

But when Benjy left the store with his package his heart almost stopped beating. There was no Tony! Tony was gone!

Benjy looked across the street. Carl lived in that house! And in his heart he knew what had happened. Carl had untied the pony!

Angrily, Benjy started on his way home. It was a long walk, but he trudged along, cutting through a field now and then and stopping often to put down his package and pick off a sandbur.

In the meantime, as Mama worked in the kitchen, she glanced out of the window. "Oh, my!" she said. She saw a riderless Tony come into the yard. "There must be trouble. Where is Benjy?"

Then Mama did what every mother would have done. She quickly put on her sweater, hurriedly told Fritzie to watch the baby for a little while, and started down the road to look for Benjy. She walked a long way, but finally, way down the road, she saw him coming. She knew it was Benjy carrying the bag of groceries.

Benjy cried a little when he came close to his mother.

"Tony is gone!" he said.

"No, no, dry your tears. Tony is not gone. Tony is at home, safe in the yard. Didn't you tie him?"

"Oh, I tied him, Mama. Someone loosened the knot. And Carl lives across the street from the store."

"I know what you think, Benjy. But you must not blame Carl, because you don't know for sure. No matter. We will find an answer. If it was Carl, then I think I know the reason why he says he doesn't like you. It is not you. It is the pony, Benjy. Carl is jealous that you have a pony and he has no pony to ride. And if that is the reason, then we must find a way to make Carl happy."

Benjy stooped to pull off some more of the sand-burs he had picked up in the field. "These prick my fingers," he said.

"They are seeds," his mother explained. "Without the prickers they would all fall to the ground and stay in one place. With prickers they catch onto your clothes and take a piggy-back ride with you until you pick them off and throw them in another place. That way they are travelers. Seeds must travel."

"But all seeds don't have prickers," Benjy said.

"Oh, no. You are right, Benjy. Some seeds are little propellers. The wind whirls them around and around like little helicopters, and they can travel far away."

Mama stopped a minute. "Wait," she said. "I will show you something else." She stepped to the edge of the field where dozens of milkweeds were growing. She picked one.

"Look at this pretty thing," she said. "It is a

seed pod that looks like a little dry, gray, dead bird. But watch now."

Mama cracked open the milkweed pod. "Look," she said. "Look how tightly all the little seeds lie in their mother's bed. Now I will pull them apart."

Squeezing some between her finger, Mama laid a little bunch in her hand and separated them. Opening her hand she let the wind do the rest. One by one they flew away until there were hundreds of them in the air.

Benjy put his groceries down and clapped his hands. "They have parachutes!" he cried.

"Yes, little parachutes to make them travel far, far away. But come, now, we must go home. But first, look for a minute across the street, and see the trees painted in sunset colors. It's God's bouquet, Benjy."

Benjy was happy to find Tony safely in the yard. He could easily have been wandering on some lonely road all alone. Benjy petted him over and over and then took him to the barn for rest and food.

Before Benjy left for school the next morning his mother had something special to say to him.

"What will you say to Carl today about the pony?"

"What should I say?" Benjy asked. "I do think it was Carl who let him loose."

"But still, you don't know for sure," Mama said. "So you must not say anything about it. One shiner is enough! But I think there is a better way—we must put sugar on the pony."

Benjy laughed hard. "But I don't want a sugar horse," he said.

"No," said Mama. "You must ask Carl to come for a pony ride."

"But he calls Tony an old nag," Benjy reminded Mama.

"Yes, I know, but he doesn't mean it," Mama said. "You'll see. He would like a pony too, and I think he would like a ride on Tony. Why don't you ask him?"

At school that morning Benjy did as his mother had said. He met Carl face to face on the schoolyard, but Carl ran away and Benjy said nothing.

At recess he stood near Carl in the entry line, so he tried a question: "Will you walk home with me tonight and have a ride on my pony?"

Carl stiffened a little and Benjy thought he was going to say no. Instead, his eyes went down and he said, softly, "I would like that."

The boys exchanged a few smiles in the classroom during the rest of the day, and after school they met at the front door.

"If I am going to ride your pony, what will you do?" Carl asked.

"Oh, we will take turns," Benjy said. "Besides, there is Little One."

"Who is Little One?" Carl asked.

"Little One is the goat," Benjy said.

"Why do you call the goat Little One?" Carl asked.

"Because he never grew quite as big as he was supposed to. But he is strong. He pulls a goat wagon. When you ride the pony I will have Little One take me for a ride. And when I ride the pony you may drive the goat."

Carl was excited and so was Benjy. Mama had cookies and milk for them and then came the riding. Carl had never been on a horse and never in his whole life had he driven a goat wagon. He shouted with glee until Benjy told him, "Be a little quieter, Carl. The animals are not used to noisy riders."

For Carl the time passed much too swiftly, and Benjy's mother called too soon.

"Time to stop playing," Mama said. "If you like, you may ride the pony to the store. But Benjy, you must come right back." And she gave them each a nickel.

"Can we both ride the pony at the same time?" Carl asked.

"Yes, we'll take the saddle off and put a blanket over Tony. There will be room," Benjy said.

Mama watched them go. "Sugar," she said. "There is nothing better to catch people with than sugar."

4 Mister Good

Fritzie felt very unhappy. "There is nothing to do, Mama," he said. "When may I go to school like Benjy does?"

"It will not be long now, Fritzie," Mama said. "Now it is spring, the beautiful spring when the whole outdoors wakes up. Then will come the summer, the time of growing things. And then, Fritzie, will come the autumn days, the time of painted leaves, and that will be school time for you. But, see, I have something for you to do now."

"What is it, Mama?" he asked.

"Look in the bowl where you have the polliwogs," Mama said. "They already have their hind legs, and it is high time they go back to the creek where they can grow into the frogs they are supposed to be. You must take them back. Papa is working near the creek and you will not be alone."

Fritzie picked up the bowl.

"Wait," Mama said. "I will give you something else," and she slipped two big sugar cookies into a bag. "There," she said. "One is for you, Fritzie, and one is for Papa." She tucked the paper sack between his fingers and the bowl.

Mama did not worry about the creek. It was only a little trickle with small pools of water here and there where the polliwogs swam. It was a wonderful playground for a boy.

At the creek Fritzie found the biggest pool and said goodbye to his polliwogs as he tipped the bowl upside down. Then he moved down the creek a little to a smaller pool, hoping to catch a new batch of polliwogs. They were hard to find, but he managed to get two of them. He put them into the bowl, scooping up some creek water, when suddenly he spied a baby turtle. It was no bigger than a twenty-five cent piece. He picked it up and its little legs moved furiously. Fritzie dropped it into the bowl with the polliwogs. It was a good catch!

He stood up and turned around. And there, quietly watching him, was a yellow wire-haired dog.

"Woof!" barked the dog.

"Woof to you," Fritzie said.

The dog wagged his tail and Fritzie went close to pet him. "Your bones are sticking out," he said to the dog, "and you look hungry. Come on, I'll give you a bite of my cookie."

Fritzie took one cookie out of the bag. The dog jumped for it.

"Don't jump!" Fritzie said. "Sit! If you sit still you will get a piece." And the yellow dog sat still. Quickly the cookie was gone.

Fritzie looked in the bag. Papa's cookie was still there. The dog made a jump and a snap for the bag, but Fritzie held it high.

"Don't jump and don't snap," he said, "and you will have a bite."

The yellow dog sat still, waiting. Fritzie broke

off a piece, then another and another and soon the whole cookie was gone.

"You are a good dog," Fritzie said. "You didn't jump much or snap when I told you not to. You are a very good dog. I will call you Mister Good. Come on, I'm going home. If you want to go along, you can meet Mama."

The dog followed, jumping against Fritzie with happiness and wagging his tail, while the creek water sloshed in the polliwog bowl.

Mama was on the back porch when Fritzie and the dog arrived.

"Oh, my!" she said. "Oh, my! I see you have found a dog!"

"No, no, Mama," Fritzie said. "The dog found me. And Mama, he listens to me, and he does what I tell him to do. So I call him Mr. Good."

"How do you do, Mr. Good?" Mama said. "You look like you have not eaten for a long time."

"He had a cookie, Mama," Fritzie said. "I gave him some of my cookie."

"And what about the other cookie, Papa's cookie? Did you bring it to Papa?"

Fritzie hung his head and looked at the ground. "No, Mama," he said. "Mr. Good ate that one too."

"That was wrong, Fritzie," Mama said. "It was very wrong. Now you will have to go back and bring Papa a cookie. It is the only right way. Here, give me the bowl of polliwogs and I will get the cookie. Oh," she said, as she looked into the bowl, "I see you have also found a turtle. That means you will have to catch flies to feed to him, Fritzie."

Papa was pleased with the cookie and he seemed pleased with Mr. Good. "He is a nice farm dog, Fritzie, but maybe he already has a home."

"But I want to keep him, Papa," Fritzie said.

"You know you can't keep him if he belongs to someone else. Maybe he just came over to play with you for a little while. But we will see. If he has a home he'll want to go back to it."

But Mr. Good had no idea of leaving. When evening came he hungrily ate all the table scraps Fritzie brought him. Besides the food he lapped up a big bowl of milk and then settled himself comfortably on the back porch.

"Where will that dog sleep tonight?" Papa asked Mama. "He can't stay outside. The nights are still pretty cold."

"In the barn," Mama said. "Not in the house. Two boys and a baby are enough in one house. We have no room for a dog."

This did not please Fritzie very much, but he knew Mama. When she said no, she meant *no*. Mama did not change her mind very often. Papa knew that, too.

So when evening came, Mr. Good went into the barn. Mama gave Fritzie an old rug. "Put it in the goat wagon," she said. "It will make a good bed and he will be out of the draft."

Mr. Good cried a little and Fritzie felt sad, but he knew there was no other way. Suddenly he remembered something. He had eaten *his* supper, and Mr. Good had been fed, but his turtle was still hungry. It was time to catch some flies. There were plenty of them around the back door, and swatting some of them was easy. Fritzie brought them to the bowl.

"Oh, Mama," he called. "Mama, what did you do with my polliwogs?"

Mama went to the bowl. The polliwogs were gone! Mama smiled.

"You are asking me what I did with the polliwogs?" Mama asked. "I think you had better ask the turtle."

And then Fritzie knew. The turtle, too, had eaten his supper. "Turtles and polliwogs can't live together," he said.

As for Mr. Good, he began to look a little better every day.

"You are getting a little fat around those bones," Papa said. "You are a good dog and we are glad you came to our house." Papa petted him gently.

"Come in for supper, Papa." It was Mama calling.

"No, Mr. Good, she is not calling you," Papa said, as the dog tried to squeeze through the doorway with him. "Mama says she will not have a dog in the house, but you will get your supper when we are finished."

The supper was especially good. Mama was a wonderful cook, and she always saw to it that Mr. Good got a fair share of the leftovers with a good amount of milk. Fritzie carried the bowl outside and Mr. Good was always waiting for it.

But one day there was no Mr. Good. Fritzie called and called. After a long time Fritzie spied him coming across the road. But Mr. Good was carrying something. It was white and it was quite big. He was running fast and looking very pleased with himself. Carefully he dropped his prize at Fritzie's feet. It was a man's white shoe.

"Mama, Mama!" Fritzie called. "Look what Mr. Good found!"

Mama came. "Oh, my. Oh, my," she said. "One shoe. And it is Mr. McCulla's shoe."

41

"How do you know, Mama?" Fritzie asked. "Are you sure?"

"Oh, I am very sure," Mama said. "I saw it Sunday at church, on Mr. McCulla's foot. I said to myself, 'Mr. McCulla, you are the only farmer with white Sunday shoes.' So, Fritzie, you must bring it back and tell him your dog is sorry, and you are sorry, too, and you hope it will not happen again."

Fritzie did not like to go back with the shoe, but he knew he had to do it. He walked very slowly to the front porch of the McCulla house, holding the shoe behind him. Sure enough! Right there on the porch was the other white shoe. Fritzie knocked on the door, and Mrs. McCulla answered.

"Why Fritzie," she said. "What brings you to my house?"

"This," Fritzie said, and he held out the shoe.

"That is Mr. McCulla's shoe," she said. "It belongs with the other one, over there. I cleaned them and put them out to dry. Where did you get it, Fritzie?"

"Mr. Good, my dog, brought it home," Fritzie said. "My mother says to tell you he is sorry and that I am sorry, too."

"That is nice, Fritzie," Mrs. McCulla said. "Mr. McCulla would not like it if one of his shoes were missing."

"My mother also says she hopes it will not happen again," Fritzie said.

"It will not happen again," Mrs. McCulla told him, "because I will keep them inside to dry after this."

That made Fritzie feel much better, and he and Mr. Good raced each other home.

But the next day was just as bad. After Fritzie

had finished his supper and brought the dog his heaping bowl of food, he found Mr. Good lying on a strange mat, a mat that had the word WELCOME written on it. He called Mama and pointed to the mat.

Mama shook her head. "Mr. Good," she said, "I think you have the wrong name. You should be called Mr. Bad."

"He is never bad when he is with me, Mama," Fritzie said. "It is only when he is alone that he does wrong things."

"Well, you have another trip to make to the McCulla's," Mama said. "It is Mrs. McCulla's mat."

"Are you sure, Mama?" Fritzie asked.

"I am very, very sure," Mama said. "Mrs. McCulla is the only farm neighbor who has a welcome mat. Bring it back and say you will try to teach your dog better manners."

Soon Fritzie was knocking on the McCulla front door. This time it was Mr. McCulla who answered and he looked angry.

"This is your mat, Mr. McCulla," Fritzie said. "My dog brought it to our house, but I will try to teach him better manners."

"I thank you for bringing it back," Mr. McCulla said, "but your dog is a thief. He does need better manners, and I hope you will teach him."

Fritzie put the rug down by the door. "We are sorry," he said and he turned and ran down the walk.

"You have been a bad dog," he said to Mr. Good. "You must not steal. Why do you do that when I am not with you? When you are alone you are Mr. Bad. When you are with me you are Mr. Good."

Once again on the back porch, Mr. Good finally

43

got his supper. Mama and Papa both came to the door.

"What did Mrs. McCulla say?" Mama asked.

"Mr. McCulla was the one who came to the door," Fritzie said.

"Well, what did Mr. McCulla say?" Mama asked.

"He said my dog was a thief and I should teach him not to be," Fritzie said.

"He is right," Mama said.

"But he never steals when I am with him," Fritzie said. "It is always when he is alone."

Papa and Mama went back into the kitchen.

"The boy is right, Mama," Papa said. "The dog is trouble when he is alone. We must try to let him in the house."

"I don't like that idea," Mama said. "Our house is already very full."

"We must try it," Papa said. "If he is trouble, then we will think of something else."

Mama agreed. "All right," she said. "Tell Fritzie to get the rug from the barn."

Fritzie could hardly believe what he heard and his legs fairly flew to the barn. Mr. Good jumped with big bounds, almost as though he understood what was happening.

"Where should I put it, Mama?" Fritzie asked. "Where is the best place?"

"In the kitchen," Mama said. "In the kitchen by the stove."

Fritzie spread it out carefully, and Mr. Good plumped himself squarely in the middle of it.

"See," Mama said. "He already thinks he owns the kitchen!"

Both Fritzie and his brother Benjy went happily

upstairs at bedtime, knowing that Mr. Good was warm and safe and happy in the house.

When Mama and Papa decided it was time for them to go to bed, Mama did what she did every night.

"I will go upstairs and make sure the boys are covered," she said.

But in a very short time she was back downstairs. She stood in front of Papa with her hands on her hips.

"Papa," she said loudly. "That does it! That really does it! I go upstairs to cover two boys and what do I find? Not two heads on the pillow, but three —three, Papa. Fritzie's and Benjy's, and in the middle the head that belongs to Mr. Good. He must go back to the barn, Papa."

Papa stood up. Slowly he shook his finger at Mama. When he did that, Mama knew his mind was made up and there was no way to change it.

"Mama," he said. "There is something you must know. In life there are certain things that go together. It has always been like that. A ring is no good without the finger to put it on. A candle needs the wick or it is worth nothing. And it is the same with a boy and his dog, Mama. They belong together."

5 To Give and To Get

Children longed to go down the private path that led to neighbor Magee's little lake, but they were afraid. "Mr. Magee is an ogre," they said. But some of Benjy's friends had been there, and had told him wonderful stories. They said big fish jumped clear out of the water, and giant bullfrogs were as big as baby rabbits, and the snapping turtles had shells as large and as round as dishpans. They said there were water lilies everywhere, of all colors, and sometimes there were woodland animals that came for a cool drink.

"It is a wonderful place, Mama," Benjy said, and he related all the stories that the boys had told him.

"It is not like that," Mama said. "I know it's not. It is only a little lake, and little lakes are full of little things. Turtles and fish do not grow very big when their home is so small. As for animals, Benjy, many times we have walked through those woods close to Magee lake. What animals did you see there?"

"Squirrels," Benjy said.

"And what else?" Mama asked.

"A woodchuck, once," Benjy answered.

46

"Yes, and that is all," Mama said. "Your friends have told you stories, Benjy; stories blown up as big as balloons. The children want to go there only because it is a private lake and they know they are not welcome. Lake Magee is a good place to stay away from, Benjy."

But the more Benjy thought about it, the more he wanted to go. Maybe the boys were right and maybe Mama was wrong. He knew about the little path that led to the lake. It was in the back of Mr. Magee's farm and was hidden by trees and bushes. He had seen the path but had never been on it. He was sure he could find the way.

Something inside of Benjy seemed to be pushing him. It was pushing him toward the lake and telling him to go, and before he knew it he was on his way. The path was overgrown with weeds and bushes but he followed the trail all the way to the lake.

"Oh," he said to himself, "it *is* small, just like Mama said. But I will sit here a while and watch." He found a quiet spot on a little rise in the ground close beside the water's edge, where one lonely white water lily snuggled its head between the lily pads. "Only one water lily," he said to himself. A baby turtle was sunning himself on an old log close by. Benjy watched for the fish to jump out of the water, but there were none. He remembered what Mama had said: "Stories, Benjy, only stories."

It was quiet and peaceful sitting there and he wished he had a fishing pole. But suddenly, there was a strong hand around his arm and a loud voice said, "You are on private property."

Benjy shivered and looked up into the angry face of Mr. Magee.

"Oh . . . oh!" he stammered. "You're the ogre!"

"I am no ogre," he said, and swinging his cane through the air he pushed Benjy toward the path. "Get out of here," he said, "and don't come back."

Benjy ran. He ran all the way home and into the safety of his mother's kitchen. Mama was busy, but she looked up as Benjy came in.

"Oh, you're sick!" she said.

"No, Mama," Benjy said. "I am not sick."

"Yes, you are," she said. "You are as white as a bed sheet."

"No, Mama, no," Benjy said.

"Then there must be another reason," Mama said. "Come, tell me."

It was no use, Benjy thought. Mama would keep asking questions until he told her what had happened.

"I was by the lake," he said.

"And neighbor Magee caught you!" said Mama.

"Yes," Benjy answered, and he started to cry.

"This is no time for tears," Mama said. "Tell me, what did Mr. Magee say to you?"

"He waved his cane at me and told me to go home and not to come back," Benjy said.

"And what did you say to him?" Mama wanted to know.

"Nothing much, Mama. Only that he must be the ogre."

"Only?" Mama said. "*Only?* Benjy, Benjy, that was wrong. Mr. Magee needed a soft answer. A soft answer will quiet an angry word. But I think there is something that Mr. Magee and Benjy should both know."

"What is that, Mama?"

"It is that we almost always get what we give. It

shouldn't be that way, but it is. If you give a boy a punch, Benjy, what will you get back?"

"A punch," Benjy said.

"And if you give a kick?"

"A kick back," said Benjy.

"Yes," Mama said. "And it is the same with a smile. You give a smile and a smile comes back. Kind words bring back kind words. You must know that, Benjy, and Mr. Magee should know it too. But you see, Benjy, this is not the end of the story. The story is not finished, and we must end it in the right way."

Benjy was fearful. "How, Mama?" he asked.

"You must go to Mr. Magee with some kind words," she said.

"No, Mama, no," Benjy cried. "I'm afraid of him."

"He will not hurt you," Mama said. "And if you say the right words he will not scold you, either."

"Will you go with me?" Benjy asked.

"Oh, no," Mama said. "When you went to the lake this afternoon you did not ask me to go along, and I will not go along now. But I will try to make it a little easier for you."

"How?" Benjy asked.

"I will give you something to bring to Mr. Magee," she said. "And then you may tell him the sorry words."

Mama sat down at the kitchen table and wrote something. She put it in an envelope and sealed it. Carefully, then, she wrapped a very big loaf of her homemade bread and tied a white ribbon around it.

"There," she said, and she handed the bread and the note to Benjy. "First give him the bread, and then tell him you are sorry you were on his property and that you called him by an ugly name. Then give him the note and tell him you will wait for an answer."

Mama watched Benjy as he walked down the road. She felt sorry for him, but she knew it was the right thing to do. Oh, how she hoped Mr. Magee would be kind and understanding.

Benjy was careful to go to Mr. Magee's back door. He knocked softly. Soon he could hear the thump, thump of Mr. Magee's cane on the wooden floor. The door opened and for a long minute the old man and the boy stood and looked at each other. Finally Benjy found his voice. He held out the loaf of bread and said, shakily, "This is a present for you, Mr. Magee. It is some of my mother's homemade bread."

The old man took the loaf. "I am grateful to your mother," he said.

"I came to say that I am sorry I was on your property this morning and that I said bad words to you."

There was just a little bit of a smile on the old man's face. Quickly Benjy thrust the note into his hand.

"I must wait for an answer to this," he said.

Mr. Magee took the bread and the note to the kitchen table. He put his glasses on and, tearing the envelope open, he read the note.

His whole face seemed to light up. He smiled broadly and came back to where Benjy was still standing in the open doorway.

"Tell your mother I will do as she asks," he said. "I will come for Sunday dinner, son. The note says at twelve o'clock and I will be on time."

"Thank you, Mr. Magee," Benjy said. Then he

turned around quickly and ran all the way home. All out of breath he pushed the kitchen door open.

"He smiled, Mama," Benjy shouted. "He smiled and he said he will come for dinner."

Mama patted Benjy's head. "It was a wrong thing that you did," she said, "but it has helped your mama to remember that an old man needs kindness too."

Benjy did not know whether he was happy to have Mr. Magee come or not. On Sunday Benjy and Fritzie watched for him from the living room window.

"He's coming, Mama," they called at last. "He's coming and he has packages; packages wrapped in newspaper."

Mr. Magee thumped his cane on the kitchen door and Papa was there to open it.

"Good morning, neighbor," Papa said.

Mr. Magee shook Papa's hand and then put all of the packages in the corner by the kitchen door. He took a deep breath. "Oh, my," he said. "It smells like my kitchen used to smell when my wife was there with me."

The dinner was as good to taste as it was to smell. There were fried chicken pieces and feather-light dumplings smothered in smooth gravy. The potatoes were whipped into mounds of whiteness and the vegetables were fresh from Papa's garden. There was homemade bread and blueberry jam from Mama's blueberry bushes, and for dessert a juicy apple pie with a big slice of cheese laid across the top.

Benjy and Fritzie ate their share of Mama's dinner, but their eyes kept straying to the funny-looking packages in the corner. They counted four of them, and wondered what Mr. Magee could be hiding in all that newspaper wrapping.

When the dinner was over and all the dishes had been washed and cleared away, Mr. Magee thought it was time for him to go home.

"Never, in all of my life, have I had a better dinner," he said, "and I am thankful to all of you."

"There are many more Sundays ahead," Mama said, "and we would be pleased to have you come and spend each one with us."

"Thank you, thank you," he said, and he reached over to pat both of the boys. "There are packages in the corner by the kitchen door," he said. "Will you get them and put them on the table? Be quick!" he said with a smile.

Benjy and Fritzie did not have to be told a second time. They scurried to the corner and laid the four packages on the table. Mr. Magee picked them up.

"There," he said. "A big one for Benjy and a big one for Fritzie. And also a little one for each, but open the big one first."

The boys could wait no longer and tugged at the newspaper, unrolling a most happy gift.

"Fishing poles!" they both cried at once.

"Quickly now, the little package," said Mr. Magee.

Benjy got his open first and found something he had never seen before. He turned it over and over.

"What is it Mr. Magee?" he asked. "What is it?" He saw that Fritzie's was the same.

"That is a fish scaler," Mr. Magee said. "Every fisherman must learn early to clean his own fish. But there is one more thing I have for you; something I could not wrap in paper."

"I think they already have enough," Papa said.

"No, they will need one more thing," he said. "And so I'm giving Lake Magee to be their fishing place for as long as they like." Turning to the boys he said, "Fish near the lily pads. That is where the fish play hide and seek. And when you young fishermen have caught enough fish, stop at the back door and say hello to a very old fisherman."

6 A Thief in the Night

The most important days of the year in Papa's house were the birthdays. There were always two celebrations. The first one, which was the real birthday, was called Choosing Day. It was the day when the birthday person could choose all the food for the whole day. He would also announce what present he would like to have. The second celebration was Present Day. That often came quite a bit later, because trips to the little town were very few and the present that had been picked was often hard to find. It was on this day that the birthday cake was served.

Today was Benjy's birthday. The day before he had told Mama what he would like for breakfast. In the morning the birthday hat was on his plate. Mama could see the excitement in Benjy's face. His cheeks were pink and his blue eyes were sparkling. Carefully he put the birthday hat on his head, and then closed his eyes while Papa said grace and thanked God for a birthday boy. Then came the food. Hot baked apples beside a stack of Mama's paper-thin pancakes were smothered in butter and swimming in the syrup from Papa's maple trees.

There was even a dessert for breakfast: ice-cold custard in the shape of a star, one point for each family member—Papa, Mama, Benjy, Fritzie, and year-old baby Lisha.

When the breakfast was over, the most exciting time came. It was time for the choosing to be made known; until that moment a very guarded secret.

"Climb on the birthday stool," Mama said. "We all want to know what your present is to be."

Benjy stood on the stool which had been placed alongside of his chair. Carefully he straightened the beautiful birthday hat, and, standing very tall, he said, "For my present, I would like a coonskin cap. Please."

Mama and Papa looked at each other. Fritzie looked troubled.

"And what," Papa asked, "is a coonskin cap? I have never heard of such a thing."

"It is a fur cap, Papa, with a tail that hangs down in the back."

"But you will look like an animal," Papa said.

"But I will not *be* an animal," Benjy answered.

"We will not know if it is Mr. Good or our Benjy coming home," said Mama.

Benjy smiled. "Mr. Good has four legs," he reminded Mama.

"I would like to know two things," said Papa. "First, where did you get an idea for this cap, Benjy, and second, where can you buy one?"

"A boy in school, named Adam, has a coonskin cap. He says his father bought it in the big city."

"But the big city is too far away," Papa said. "Well, we will see. But you must remember, as always, Benjy, if we cannot find the chosen thing you will have to make a second choice. But we will try. We will try very hard."

And Papa did try very hard. The country store-keeper had never had a coonskin cap on his shelf. "I have good stocking caps," he said. "And I have warm woolen helmets, but coonskin caps? No. No one has ever asked for a coonskin cap. Maybe you will have to go to the big city."

"Oh, but I can't do that," Papa said. "To go to the big city I'd have to take a train, and I simply can't make such a long trip just for a cap."

But Mama had an idea. "We will not say no to Benjy yet," she said. "I will write to a mail-order house. Maybe they will be able to send us a coon-skin cap."

The very next morning the mail order was in Mama's mailbox by the side of the road, ready for the mailman to pick up. By afternoon the train was carrying it to the big city.

"We will forget about it for now," Mama said. "It may be a few weeks before we get an answer. If there is no coonskin cap, Benjy will have to choose again."

Papa's work went on as always. The crops had all been harvested, but there were still cows to milk, a few pigs and some chickens to feed, and eggs to gather.

"Come, Fritzie," Papa said one Saturday morn-ing. "Benjy has always helped me gather the eggs, but you are a schoolboy now and your hands must learn to work too. Many hands make a heavy load light."

Mr. Good hopped along beside them, but near to the hen-house he caught the scent of something strange. As soon as they were inside of the hen-house, Papa knew the reason.

"Oh, my. Oh, my," he said. "There are feathers everywhere! And oh, see, that's not all. Look at the eggshells! We have had a thief in the night!"

"Not Mr. Good, Papa. It wasn't Mr. Good."

"I know that, Fritzie. Mr. Good was in the house. But a thief was here. A thief who likes chickens and eggs. A stray dog, maybe, or even an animal running wild."

"There is a little red fox in the corn field by the creek," Fritzie said.

"How do you know?" Papa asked.

"I see him there," Fritzie said.

"Well, whoever is stealing our eggs, we will have to get rid of him," Papa said.

"How will you get rid of him?" Fritzie asked.

"I still have old trusty, the gun," Papa said.

"Oh, Papa, don't shoot the little red fox," Fritzie cried. "He is Mr. Good's playmate."

"How do you know that?" Papa asked.

"Because I see it almost every day. They play a game of tag between the corn stalks."

"And where does the little red fox live?" Papa asked.

"I don't know," Fritzie said. "Mr. Good always finds him. Don't kill the little red fox, Papa. Mr. Good will be sad."

"And so will a little boy named Fritzie," Papa said. "But I will not go looking for him. I will guard the hen-house. Whoever the thief is, he will be in trouble with your Papa and his gun."

"But the red fox doesn't know any better, Papa. He doesn't know it is wrong to steal, and he must get hungry."

"I know that," Papa said. "All wild animals need to find their own food. But the place to look for it is not in my hen-house. But come now, we will gather the eggs that are left and take them to Mama."

Mama was reading a letter. "It is from the mail-order house," she said. "Benjy will be disappointed. They have no coonskin caps."

Papa shrugged his shoulders. "Then he must choose something else," he said. "But look, Mama. We do not have as many eggs as usual. There has been a thief in the hen-house."

"How can you be sure?" Mama asked.

"By the feathers and the eggshells," Papa said.

"What will you do about it?" Mama asked.

Papa was watching Fritzie and knew he was ready to cry. He thought it best not to talk about the gun, so he said to Mama, "We will wait and see. Maybe he won't come back."

"As for Benjy's birthday present, I think we must try once more," Mama said. "There is still another mail-order house. Today I will send another letter."

Everyone was quiet at the supper table. Benjy was disappointed about his cap, Papa was worried about the chickens, Fritzie could think only about the little red fox, and Mama seemed to have no one to talk to.

"I think everyone needs an early bed tonight," Mama said. Later, when she helped Fritzie with his night clothes, there were tears in his eyes.

"Why are you crying?" she asked.

"For the little red fox, Mama," Fritzie said. "Papa is going to shoot the little red fox."

"Papa will shoot him only if he steals eggs in the hen-house," Mama said. "And then, Fritzie, it will need to be done. You must learn that there are some things in life that we do not like to do, but we must do them just the same. Our lives are not only filled with happy times. There are sad times, too. And it helps to try to think happy things, Fritzie. So go to bed now and put the little red fox away. Think of—well, think of Papa and his tractor. I will ask him if he will let you ride with him tomorrow."

Long after the children were asleep, Papa and Mama talked about them and the farm. Suddenly Mama sat up straight.

"Listen!" she said. "Listen, Papa! There is squawking in the hen-house."

Quickly Papa was on his feet and into his jacket. Taking the gun from its secret hiding place, he dashed out the door.

Mama waited for what seemed like a very long time. Papa would be coming back again any minute, she thought. But as she watched the door waiting for him, she heard it. There was one loud bang.

"That was a gunshot!" she said aloud. "Oh, my poor Fritzie! He will cry again for his little red fox."

Soon Papa came in the door. His face was flushed and he wore the biggest smile Mama had ever seen.

"I got him, Mama," he said. "Just with one bullet I got him. Come quickly and see."

Mama got up very slowly and went to the door. "It is good for the hen-house," she said, "but it is sad for Fritzie."

Papa kept right on smiling. "Oh, no, Mama, you have a surprise coming," he said. He pointed to a little mound on the back porch. "See," he said, "the feathers are still in his claws."

Mama blinked. "It . . . is . . . not a red fox," she said, slowly.

The porch was lighted only by the open kitchen door. Mama looked at Papa. "What is it?" she asked.

Papa fairly shouted. "A raccoon, Mama. It is a raccoon!"

Mama was relieved. "Oh, I am glad," she said. "It will be good news for Fritzie in the morning."

But Papa shouted louder. "Mama," he said. "Is that all you can see? Is it only a dead raccoon that you see? It is more, Mama, much much more! It is Benjy's birthday present! It is Benjy's coonskin cap!"

Suddenly Mama understood. She clapped her hands. "Papa," she said. "That is what it will be! Just how it will all come about, I do not know. But somehow it will become a coonskin cap."

"I will take it to Mr. Todman in the morning before the children are awake," Papa said. "He is the man who skins the deer for the hunters and tans the hides. I will have him take care of the raccoon."

"And I will get busy with the sewing," Mama said. "I will measure Benjy's woolen school cap and make a fine, warm lining. Around the lining I will sew the fur. And, as Benjy says, the tail must hang in the back."

Papa was busy and Mama was busy and before another week had passed, the coonskin cap was finished. It was beautiful.

Fritzie said little more about the red fox, only that he was still down by the creek and that he and Mr. Good still played games every day.

"It is time now for Benjy to get his present,"

Mama said to Papa. "I will make the birthday cake when he is in school today and at supper time we will have Present Day.

The table was filled with many good things. "Tonight we have everything I like," Benjy said. "Chicken and everything that's good."

When the main course was finished, Mama brought out the birthday cake, as she and Papa sang the happy birthday song.

Benjy jumped up and stood beside his chair.

"But the present, Mama," he cried. "The present is not here."

"The present *is* here," Mama said. "Please, Papa, will you get the present?"

Papa disappeared into the living room and came back with the coonskin cap on his head.

Benjy screamed, "You got it! You got it! A coonskin cap! Where did you get it?"

Papa took it off and put it on Benjy's head. "Sit down," he said, "and I will tell you the story."

The children listened, open-mouthed, as Papa told the whole tale of the raccoon who was a thief.

When Papa had finished, Benjy said, "Thank you, Mama," and "Thank you, Papa," over and over again. Fritzie added, "I told you, Papa, the little red fox was not a thief."

Bedtime came all too soon, but both boys were tired and sleep found them very quickly.

Mama sat with Papa in the living room. "It has been a happy day," she said, "but a very busy day. I am tired, too."

"I will go upstairs tonight and do the tucking in," Papa said. "You stay here and sit quietly."

But very soon Papa was back on the stairway. "Mama," he said in a loud whisper. "Mama, you must come here and see." Papa was shaking with laughter. "This you cannot miss," he said.

Mama and Papa stood together beside the boys' bed. Both of them clapped their hands over their mouths to keep from laughing aloud. There was Benjy, with the covers drawn tightly around his neck, and on his head was the coonskin cap.

"I told you," Mama whispered. "I told you that we would not be able to tell our Benjy from Mr. Good."

7 Give Yourself

"You are home later than usual," Mama said to Benjy and Fritzie when they came home from school.

"We stopped at Robbie's house," Benjy explained. Robbie goes to our school and he asked us to see where he lives."

"You have never talked about Robbie," Mama said. "Is he a new boy in your school?"

"Oh, no, Mama," Benjy said. "He has been there all along, but he never takes part in our games."

"And why is that?" Mama asked.

"He just says that he doesn't want to play," Benjy said.

"Then what does he do during recess?" Mama asked.

"Nothing," Benjy said. "He stands by the school and watches while we play."

"That isn't good," Mama said. "Every boy needs to play. Doesn't he play with his brothers and sisters?"

"He has no brothers or sisters," Benjy said.

"Oh," Mama said, "then that is the reason. He has not learned how to play, and he is afraid to join in."

63

"Maybe," Benjy said.

"We should ask him to come here sometime during summer vacation so he can play with you and with Fritzie," Mama said.

"Oh, no, Mama," Benjy said. "He wouldn't be any fun."

"Benjy! Can't you make some fun for a lonely boy?" Mama asked.

"I could," Fritzie said. "He could play with me."

"That sounds better, Fritzie," Mama said. "Benjy doesn't know that we can't always take everything for ourselves. We must sometimes give ourselves away for a while."

Mama said no more, but she knew that before long Fritzie would be having another playmate.

When that day came Fritzie was ready.

"What will you do today?" Mama asked before Robbie arrived.

Benjy said nothing. But Fritzie had been thinking.

"First, Robbie will have a ride in the goat wagon," he said. "I will show him the farm, because Robbie's father does not work their farm. Mr. Good will go with us. And we will go to the creek and look at the duck who sits on her nest." Just then an old car drove into the yard and Robbie's father let him out.

Fritzie ran out to meet him, but Benjy held back. Suddenly he realized that he would have no one to play with all day, so half-heartedly he went to join the other two. Mama was watching him.

"I'm glad, Benjy," was all she said.

Little One, the goat, was happy to be brought from the barn. He was willingly hitched to the goat wagon and Robbie smiled happily as he jogged along in the cart. But when they reached the fenced-in field where the cows grazed and where Little One usually spent his daytime hours, he refused to take another step.

"You are a stubborn goat," Fritzie said. "Unhitch him, Benjy. Put him in the pasture and we will be the goat. We will pull the wagon."

Benjy scowled. Being a goat was not his idea of fun, but he dared not say so as long as Robbie was there. Together the brothers pulled the wagon, and when they got to the creek Fritzie stopped.

"Wait," he said. "There is a mama duck here, Robbie. Every day she sits on her eggs, waiting for them to hatch. Oh, but she's gone!" he shouted. "And the eggs are gone, too."

The boys went to the nest.

"The eggs are hatched," Benjy said. "See! Only the empty shells are left."

Sure enough! Farther down the creek they could see the mama duck and four little yellow ducklings, all pecking for food in the long grasses that bordered the creek.

"We should leave her alone today," Benjy said. "She will be afraid for her children if we come too close."

Benjy was ready to accept Fritzie as the leader for the day, although usually it was the other way around. "Where do we go next?" he asked.

"To the corn field," Fritzie said. "Maybe Mr. Good can find the little red fox for Robbie."

Indeed, Mr. Good could find him! Three loud barks and the little red fox seemed to come from nowhere.

"Watch, Robbie," Fritzie said. "They play games together."

"They are trying to catch each other by the tail," Robbie said. "Do they bite each other?"

"No, never," Fritzie said. "They always play the same games. But, come on, Mr. Goat," he said to Benjy. "Pull the wagon. We will take our rider to Strawberry hill."

"And what can we do there?" Benjy asked.

"We will pick some strawberries," Fritzie said. "Maybe Mama will make us a shortcake for supper."

Robbie had never picked a strawberry in his life, but the boys were good teachers. "Look," Benjy said as he picked a beautiful dark red berry. "They must be red all over, with no white spot at the tip, just like this one."

"Where do we put them?" Robbie asked.

"In the goat wagon," Fritzie said.

"Then where will I sit?" Robbie wanted to know.

"You will not sit," Fritzie said. "On the way back you will be a goat, too, and you will help pull the wagon. Everyone must have a turn."

Suddenly Robbie screamed. "A snake, a snake." He ran to Fritzie for help.

"It is only a blue racer," Fritzie said.

"Will he bite?" Robbie asked.

"Well . . . yes, sometimes. If you get him in a corner he might bite, Papa says. But he is not a poisonous snake. The bite will be something like a bee sting."

Robbie went back to his picking spot. Soon the bottom of the goat wagon was covered with beautiful red strawberries and the trip home began. It did not seem very far going back home, because the load was not as heavy and there was an extra goat to pull the wagon.

The boys stopped at the pasture gate and Benjy

whistled for Tony the pony. He came on the run, eager for the little hands that always petted him.

"Whose pony is he?" Robbie asked.

"Mine," Benjy said. "I earned him myself. Come on, let's go to the barn and you can see where he sleeps at night."

The barn was a wonderful place, Robbie thought to himself. It was clean and there was the good smell of hay.

"I see a lot of cats," Robbie said.

"They are barn cats," Benjy said.

"What are barn cats?" Robbie wanted to know.

"Barn cats live only in the barn and do not come into the house. They catch the mice in the barn. They come to the back porch for their milk when Papa finishes with the milking. Someday soon Benjy will begin to help Papa milk the cows, and I will do Benjy's old chores. I will feed the chickens and gather the eggs and pick the garden vegetables. Mama always says that little hands have to learn early to get used to the work that big hands have to do. Do you do chores, Robbie?"

"No," Robbie said. "On our farm there is nothing to do."

"Everyone works at our house," Fritzie said. "All except the baby. Do you ever help your mother, Robbie?"

"No," he said.

"Tell her sometime that you will help her," Fritzie said. "She will be surprised and she will like it. But, come on now, let's bring the strawberries home."

Mama was surprised.

"I was wishing for a strawberry shortcake," she said, "and there are enough strawberries to cover

67

a big one. Maybe Robbie will stay for supper and help us eat it."

Robbie's big smile was answer enough.

"We will tell your father when he comes home from his work at the tannery that you are going to stay and that Fritzie's Papa will bring you home."

The supper was plain. It was only strawberry shortcake and milk. Mama made the shortcake in round cake pans. When they were baked, she put the layers on top of each other with the sweetened strawberries between each layer. Then she cut large wedge-shaped pieces, laid them on big plates, covered them with more strawberries, and then piled them high with the cream she had skimmed from the top of the milk and whipped. To Robbie it looked like a shortcake mountain! As Mama gave him a second piece and filled his milk glass for the second time, she was sure that it would help to make those thin little legs stronger.

Toward the end of the supper, Papa looked up from his plate and toward the kitchen screen door.

"Oh, my," he said. "We have more company. We have another visitor."

All the heads turned quickly and there, quietly watching them, was a baby raccoon.

"I think I am looking at another coonskin cap," Papa said. "One for Fritzie, maybe."

"Oh, no," Fritzie said. "I like a pet to be alive. I do not want him dead on my head. But look, he is asking for his supper. May I feed him? What do raccoons eat?"

"Eggs and chickens," Papa said.

Mama smiled. "We will give this one bread and milk," she said. "Maybe that will keep him away from the hen-house."

"May I bring it to him?" Fritzie asked.

"Yes," Mama said, "But don't scare him. To be friends with a raccoon you must act like a raccoon. Walk on all fours, and creep softly."

Fritzie did as he was told, but when he pushed the screen door open, the little fellow was frightened and ran off the porch. Fritzie clicked his tongue ever so softly and held out the food. Slowly, very slowly, the raccoon came back. Gingerly he took the bread and dipped it into the milk before he ate it. When it was all gone he scampered away.

"He will be back," Mama said. "Once you feed a raccoon he will be your friend forever. He will learn fast."

"He will also learn that Papa has a gun if he gets into the hen-house," Papa said.

"He will not have to go there if we feed him every day," Fritzie said.

All the while Robbie had been watching with big eyes.

"I wish he had come to my house," he said. "I don't have a pet."

"Well," Papa said, "if you don't have a pet, then it is high time for you to have one. We will tame this one for you. That must be done first. Otherwise we will never be able to catch him. But, Robbie, do you have a cage?"

"No, sir," he said.

Benjy was a quick thinker. "The empty rabbit hutch is still in the barn," he said. "It was big enough for a whole rabbit family, Papa."

"That will do just fine," Papa said. "When Robbie's raccoon is tame enough to catch, we will bring him to live at Robbie's house. He will come complete with a cage."

"Robbie is happy," Mama said. "His smile is as big as a pumpkin face," and she patted him on the shoulder. "But come now, it is time for Papa to take you home."

Robbie did not go home empty-handed. On the front seat of the truck Mama put a box of strawberries, a fruit jar filled with blueberries that she had canned the summer before, and a lot of fresh vegetables from Papa's garden.

"You must come again soon," she said. "Saturday is market day and Sunday is a church day, but any other day of the week will be fine."

Robbie said thank you for the happy day and, looking at Mama, he asked, "Will you remember about my new pet?"

"It is a promise," she said, "and Mama never breaks a promise."

When the truck drove away, Mama looked at Benjy.

"How do you feel about today?" she asked.

"Warm inside, Mama," Benjy said.

Mama nodded her head. "It comes," she said, "from giving yourself away."

8 Five Pennies' Worth

Fritzie came into the house and unhappily threw his report card on the table.

"It is not a good report card," he said to Mama.

"And how do you know that?" Mama asked. "You can't read."

"Benjy says so," he said.

Mama turned to Benjy. "And what gives you the right to open your brother's report card?" Mama asked.

"Well, I can open my own!" Benjy said.

"That is quite different," Mama replied. "What the teacher writes on your report card is for you, your Papa, and your Mama. But Fritzie's is not for you to open. Will you remember that the next time?"

"Yes, Mama," Benjy said.

"And now let me have a look at Fritzie's card," she said.

Mama read it carefully.

"It is *not* a bad card," she said as she looked at Benjy. "All the marks are good except in arithmetic. And it only says that Fritzie needs extra help at home. Well, that is something Fritzie will get. We will begin tomorrow after school. Instead of Benjy going to the store and counting change, it will be Fritzie's turn for a while."

The next afternoon Mama was ready. She had a whole cup full of money.

"Now," she said. "Put one of your hands on the table, Fritzie, and spread your fingers. How many do you have on that hand?"

Fritzie counted them. "Five fingers," he said.

"That is right," Mama answered. "And now, do you know how many people we have in our family?"

Fritzie knew that without counting. "Five people," he said.

"That is right, too," Mama said. "Five fingers on one hand and five people in our family. And today I need some doughnuts from the store," she said.

Mama put some nickels on the table. "One doughnut costs one nickel," she said. "Now spread your fingers very wide, Fritzie."

Mama laid a nickel at the end of each finger.

"There," she said. "If the five people in your family each get a doughnut, how many nickels will you need?"

"Five," Fritzie said.

"That is right," Mama answered.

Carefully she picked up five more nickels and laid them, one at a time, ahead of the other five.

"Now how many nickels do you have?" she asked.

Fritzie counted. "Ten nickels," he said.

"That is good," Mama said. "So if five people each get two doughnuts, how many doughnuts must you ask for?"

"As many as the nickels. Ten doughnuts," Fritzie said.

"That is exactly right," Mama said, and she picked up the nickels and wrapped them snugly in a piece of paper.

"Now put them in your pocket," she said, "and see what a good delivery boy you can be."

Fritzie started down the road. It seemed like a long way to the store. He stopped to talk to a little black squirrel, but the squirrel was not very friendly. Close to the store a rabbit darted from the side of the road. Fritzie chased him, but the rabbit's legs were faster than Fritzie's.

Once inside the store, Fritzie reached into his pocket for the package of nickels. The wrapper was partly open and some of the nickels were loose in his pocket. One by one he took them out and laid them in front of his fingers, just as Mama had done. But his thumb had only one nickel instead of two.

The storekeeper came to help him, and smiled at the way Fritzie had arranged the nickels at the end of his fingers.

"What must you buy?" he asked.

"Ten doughnuts," Fritzie answered.

"You will need one more nickel," the storekeeper said.

Fritzie felt in his pocket. "Mama gave me ten nickels," he said, "but one is missing." The pocket was empty.

"Did you run or did you walk?" the storekeeper asked.

Fritzie thought a minute.

"I chased a rabbit," he said.

"And I think one nickel hopped out when you

did that," the storekeeper said. "Tell me, how many doughnuts will nine nickels buy?"

"Nine doughnuts," Fritzie said.

"You are right," said the storekeeper, and he put nine doughnuts into a paper bag.

"How much is a licorice whip?" Fritzie asked.

"One penny," said the storekeeper.

"I do not have a penny," Fritzie said.

Suddenly he spied a group of masks on the shelf. It was close to Halloween.

"How much are the funny faces?" he asked.

"Two cents apiece," said the storekeeper.

"But I don't have two cents," Fritzie said, sadly.

Then he remembered that he had been gone a long time and that it was still a long walk home. He left the store, and for a short way he half walked and half ran toward home. Suddenly, he stopped. There was something shiny in the road.

"A nickel," he said aloud. "I found a nickel!"

He picked it up and quickly turned around and went back to the store.

The storekeeper looked surprised. "You are back again!" he said.

"I found a nickel in the road!" Fritzie said. "Shining between the stones, there was a nickel. How many pennies are there in a nickel?"

"Five," the storekeeper said.

"I will change the nickel for five pennies," Fritzie said.

The storekeeper made the change.

"There," Fritzie said. "There is one penny for a licorice whip. And here are two pennies for a funny face, and then the other two pennies are for . . . a . . . a . . . for another funny face."

"I think maybe you should buy another doughnut for your mother," the storekeeper said.

"Oh, no," Fritzie said. "It is my nickel. It is the nickel I found."

The storekeeper took some of the funny faces from the shelf and laid them on the counter. Fritzie looked each one over carefully and finally chose a devil face and a pirate face. They were soft and airy so he folded them carefully and put one in each pocket. He took a big bite of the licorice whip and started for home. On the way he began to wonder what Mama would say, but, after all, it was he who had found the nickel and he was sure that he could spend it as he liked.

When he got home, Mama took the paper bag from Fritzie.

"Now we will see how well you can count," she said. "Count with me, Fritzie."

Mama took the doughnuts out, one at a time, and put them into the doughnut jar.

"Nine," they counted, and Mama reached into the bag for number ten. But there were no more.

"Only nine doughnuts, Fritzie?" she asked. "Only nine? You had money enough for ten."

"I only had money for nine," Fritzie said. "The storekeeper said that maybe one nickel hopped out of my pocket when I chased the rabbit."

"Come here," Mama said. "I will check your pockets."

She reached into the first pocket and pulled out the pirate face.

"Oh, my," she said. "What do we have here?"

"Only a funny face, Mama," Fritzie said.

Mama felt in the other pocket.

"This pocket has a hole in it," Mama said. Then she pulled out the devil face.

Mama was horrified.

"Fritzie, Fritzie, you spent the doughnut money for this?" she asked.

Benjy was watching. "You have also a black tongue," he said to Fritzie.

"That was the licorice whip," Fritzie said. "I did not spend your money, Mama. It was my money that I spent. On the way home I found a nickel in the road."

"Did you not stop to think that it was Mama's nickel you lost and that it was Mama's nickel you found?" Mama asked. "Why did you not go back and buy the tenth doughnut?"

"That is what the storekeeper said," Fritzie told her.

"Well," Mama said, "we will put the faces away until Papa comes home. Then we will let him decide what we must do."

But Papa was not as stern as Mama. He thought it was all a little bit funny.

"Do not be too hard on Fritzie," he said. "And do not take the funny faces away. Give him a doughnut tonight for supper, but tomorrow in his school lunch he must go without. Give a doughnut to Benjy but not to Fritzie."

Later that night, Fritzie had a favor to ask.

"May I take the funny faces to school, Mama?" he asked.

"And why should you want funny faces at school?" Mama said.

"To show and to tell," Fritzie answered.

"And what could you tell about the devil face?" Mama wanted to know.

"Nothing," Fritzie said. "But I could take the pirate face."

"And what is a pirate?" Mama asked.

"Oh, a pirate is a thief," Fritzie said.

"So, when the raccoon came as a thief to Papa's hen-house, was he a pirate?" Mama asked.

"No, no, Mama," Fritzie said. "Only people are pirates, not animals."

"Then if Fritzie went to Mr. McCulla's house and took sweet cherries from his cherry tree, would Fritzie be a pirate?"

"N . . . o . . . o," Fritzie said.

"I think that if you are going to tell about pirates you had better go to Papa and ask him to take down the big red book and read to you. He will read all about the pirates and then you will have something to tell. Then you will be a good little teacher."

Fritzie listened carefully as Papa read from the encyclopedia, and when he was finished Fritzie knew much about the pirates and was sure he could tell it in school.

Sunday came and the boys were ready to go to the church. Waiting for Mama and Papa, Fritzie played with his funny faces. And when Papa called that all was ready, he stuffed the devil face in his pocket.

The time in church was always long to Fritzie. The minister's praying was especially long and Fritzie sometimes peeked a little. Today he felt in his pocket for the peppermint Papa usually gave him. And there was the funny face. He looked at Mama. Her eyes were closed, so he quietly took out the devil face and put it on. He peeked at the minister through the slits of the eyes. Then he snuggled up against Mama's arm. It was not long before Fritzie was fast asleep.

The sermon followed the praying. Mama listened, but she noticed that the minister often looked her way, and when he did a smile always came on his face. The girls behind Mama snickered and when Mama turned her head to look a little angrily at them she caught sight of Fritzie. Mama almost fainted! She grabbed the funny face and tucked it beneath her skirt. How she would liked to have spanked Fritzie, but the church was no place for that. She squeezed his arm and shook him. Fritzie awoke and felt for the funny face. It was gone. "Uh-oh," he thought, "I'm in a lot of trouble."

When the service was over, Mama thought about going out the back door so she would not have to shake the minister's hand, but she knew that would not be right. She guessed that it was her turn to say she was sorry. But to her surprise, the minister shook her hand warmly.

Laughing aloud, he said, "The church had a very strange visitor this morning."

Mama's face got very red.

"Don't be angry," the minister said. "It was only boy's play."

"That may be," Mama said, "but sometimes play can go too far. Besides, church is not the place for playing!" Mama's tone of voice told Fritzie that a spanking was in store for him.

Fritzie feared all the way home. Papa's spankings were not always easy, but he remembered that Papa never used a stick or a whip. Papa always said, "Spanking must be done with the hand so that the hand can feel when the bottom has had enough." That was a comfort to Fritzie.

But Mama had another idea after the spanking was over. When they had changed their clothes

Fritzie watched her gather a big pile of kindling wood. When it was burning brightly she called to Fritzie.

"It is time for you to get the funny faces," she said.

Fritzie brought them, walking very slowly.

"Now you will throw them both into the fire," Mama said.

Fritzie dared not say no. One at a time the funny faces went into the fire. Slowly the pirate face crumpled and burned into ashes. But the wind caught the burning devil face and carried it up the chimney, high into the tree tops above the farm.

"Oh, my," Mama said. "See that! The devil wants no part of the fire. Even the devil finds that the fire is too hot."

9 The Contest

"The school carnival will be in a few more weeks, Mama," Benjy said. "Will we go again this year?"

"Always, Benjy. We have never yet missed a school carnival. It will mean a lot of baking in the kitchen again. There will be many good smells, but the food will all be going out of the kitchen door to the baked goods sale."

"There will be some new things this year, the teacher told us," Benjy said.

"What new things?" Mama asked.

"For all the fathers, there will be an auction of used farm tools. It will help the people who no longer want to work their farms and who go to work in the city. The school will get part of the money from the sale. And for the children there will be a contest—with a *prize!*"

"A contest?" Mama asked. "What kind of a contest?"

"A contest to write a story or a poem," Benjy said.

"Do you like to write stories and poems, Benjy?" Mama asked.

"Not stories so much, but I like words that fit together and sound alike, like a poem," Benjy said.

"Those are rhyming words, Benjy," Mama said. "But poems do not always have rhyming words. Alone they do not make a poem. When I say, 'There is a mouse in the house,' I have two rhyming words, but that is not a poem. A poem is a picture made with words. When an artist paints a picture he uses brushes and paint. But a poet makes a picture with a pen and pretty words. He makes words talk."

"Oh," Benjy said. But Mama knew he did not understand, so she thought she had better explain a little more.

"You see, Benjy," she said, "when an artist sees something beautiful that he wants to paint, like a certain tree with golden leaves, he takes his easel, his chair, his brushes, and his paints, and he goes to sit near that tree. It is the same with someone who writes a poem. If he wants to write about a brook, he goes to the brook, unless of course he has been there so many times before that he knows all about it. Poets need eyes that see and ears that hear things that other people do not see and hear, and then with a pen he puts it all on paper."

"I don't understand how, Mama," Benjy said.

"All right. We will go somewhere and use our eyes and our ears," Mama said. "And we will talk about it. Maybe that will help you to write a poem."

The very next afternoon, while Papa took care of Lisha and Fritzie for awhile, Mama and Benjy had the whole time for themselves.

"Where shall we go?" Mama asked.

"To Lake Magee," Benjy said. "It is pretty there. I can even throw a fishing line into the lake."

Together they sat on the little knoll which was Benjy's favorite spot. Benjy put a worm on his hook and swished the line into the water.

"Now forget about the pole, Benjy," Mama said, "and open your ears. I hear something. Do you hear it?"

"That is a tree toad singing, Mama. I always hear him when I am here. He lives high in that tree," and Benjy pointed to the top of the tallest tree.

Just then, a blue-tailed dragonfly came to rest on the tip of Benjy's fishing pole.

"Oh, he is beautiful," Mama said. "See! You can look right through his wings. His wings are thin, like paper."

Benjy wiggled his pole and the dragonfly flew away.

"I will throw my line near the lily pads," he said.

"See how wide the water lilies are open," Mama said. "They are catching the sun. Pretty soon, when the sun goes down, they will close their petals and go to sleep."

Mama and Benjy sat there a long time, talking about all the pretty things around them, until Mama said it was time to go home.

"Now, you must remember what you saw, Benjy," she said. "Put it in your head, then let it turn around and around in there for a while. Soon you will want to write it all down. But remember that a poem is pretty talk."

For many days all kinds of words whirled through Benjy's head. When the writing day came at school he was quite ready. The classroom was very quiet. Some of the children wrote fast and long while others were finished in just a few minutes. Mr. Warson collected the papers.

"I will read them and correct your mistakes," he said, "and tomorrow we will copy them on a new sheet."

The next day, Mr. Warson took a bundle of paper from his drawer. The children gasped. There were papers in all the colors of the rainbow! They had never seen papers like these before, and they were each allowed to choose a color. Benjy could hardly wait for Mr. Warson to get to him, for in all that pile there was only one blue paper.

"It's the color of a lake," he thought. It was just the right color for his poem. When the teacher finally got to him, Benjy said, with a big sigh of relief, "May I have the blue one, please, Mr. Warson?"

He copied the poem he had written. He copied it carefully and without a mistake, thinking of the prize he might win. But there would be only one prize, and just what the prize was was still a secret.

"We copied our stories and poems today, Mama," Benjy said when he came home from school. "My poem is on a blue paper. It is on the only blue paper the teacher had."

"And what is the poem about, Benjy?" Mama asked.

"It's a secret, Mama," Benjy said. "Mr. Warson says it is best to keep it all a surprise."

"Oh, that is good," Mama said. "And if it is to be a secret you must keep it secret. Never tell a secret, because people will soon know that they cannot trust you with their secrets if you tell about others. And, Benjy, did you remember to make pretty talk?"

"I tried," Benjy said. "You will read it on carnival day, Mama. All of the poems and stories will be tacked on the wall."

"Do you think you made a good poem?" Mama asked.

"I don't know," Benjy said. "I tried hard."

"That is all that matters," Mama said. "We ask no more than that you do your best. That is enough."

Carnival day was a busy day at the school. All day long, mothers and fathers brought armloads of all kinds of things. There were farm tools, baked goods, wrapped packages, odds and ends from farm attics, vegetables, popcorn, and gallons of ice cream.

The children were excited and hard to manage, and the teachers couldn't wait for the bells to ring, especially that last bell that would send the children home. With a whoop and a cry the children were out the door, anxious to get home to get their chores finished so they could get ready for the carnival.

"Do you think Mr. Magee could ride in the truck with us?" Benjy asked Mama.

"Mr. Magee never goes anywhere. You know that, Benjy. He goes only to the store when he needs food."

"But, maybe, if I asked him, he would go," Benjy said.

"You may ask him," Mama answered, "but I think you can expect him to say no."

And Mr. Magee did say no.

"Oh, but you will like it," Benjy said. "I wrote a special poem and I think you will like to read it."

"All right, Benjy," he said. "For you I will go."

Benjy clapped his hands. "Papa will pick you up in the truck," he said.

Mr. Magee was ready long before Papa arrived.

The front seat was wide enough for Papa, Mama, baby Lisha, and Mr. Magee, and that left the whole back part of the truck for Benjy and Fritzie. They sat in the middle of the baked goods and the hand-knitted things that Mama had made.

The school was a busy place, and people went from room to room. Every room had something different. There was a fish pond where children could try to catch a present. In another room a lady from the city was drawing pictures of the children. There was a cake-walk, a guessing room, a jelly-bean game room, a popcorn room, a room for cold drinks, hot coffee, and barbeque buns, with little pots of baked beans.

"The school doesn't smell like the school," Benjy said. "I wish it was always like this."

"Then it would no longer be a school," Mama said. "If you like to have good smells when you study so much, then you'll have to do your homework in the kitchen every day."

The last event of the evening was the giving of the prize for the contest.

"What is the prize going to be?" everyone was asking, but nobody knew. The secret had been well kept.

The largest room in the school was set up with chairs packed closely together. The front of the room was drapery-covered, and behind the draperies were the stories and poems.

Benjy sat between Mama and Mr. Magee, with Papa, Fritzie, and Lisha on the other side of Mama.

"Do you think I might win?" Benjy whispered to Mama.

"That is something I do not know," Mama said. "If you win, Benjy, you will be happy for Benjy.

85

If somebody else wins, you must be happy for him."

The principal walked to the front of the crowded room. In his hand he carried a yellow envelope.

"You are all wondering about the contest," he said. "This is something the children have worked especially hard for, and they have thought about it a great deal. So in that sense everyone is a winner. And I must say that the children's stories are very good, and so are the poems."

Slowly the principal opened the draperies. There were the stories and the poems, some with a blue ribbon, others with a red or yellow one, and some with no ribbon at all.

Benjy sat up straight and craned his neck.

"My blue paper, Mama," he whispered. "My blue paper is not even there." A tear trickled down his cheek.

"Look again," Mama said. "Look carefully."

Benjy looked. But, wait! The principal was talking again.

"The prize tonight," he said, "goes to a boy—to a boy who understands a little what poetry is all about."

He opened the yellow envelope and carefully pulled out a paper. And the paper was blue!

"The winner tonight," he said, "is Benjy Erickson. Benjy, will you come and read your poem?"

Oh, how the people clapped!

And now a tear trickled down Mama's face. Benjy was on his feet, passing Mama, but for a short minute she held him back.

"Wait," she whispered loudly. "You must read it slowly, and be sure you talk plenty loud. If people cannot hear you, you might as well not get up there at all. Remember!"

Benjy smiled and ran to the front of the room. The principal patted his head and handed him the blue paper.

In a very loud voice, almost too loud, he began.

"The name of my poem," he said, "is, At Lake Magee." He waited a minute and then read on:

"There was a day when I went fishing
And all the time I kept on wishing
A fish would come and bite my hook.
I saw a treetoad that could sing,
And a dragonfly with a peekaboo wing,
But not a single fish was there.
A water-lily opened wide,
As if it tried and tried to hide
The fish that played around it.
I caught no fish, so I went home,
But with my heart I caught a poem
On the shore of Lake Magee."

The people clapped loud and long. Fritzie whistled. Mama and Papa sat stiff and straight, but their faces were all smiles.

And what was the prize? There it came down the aisle, straight from the back to the front of the room. And surprise of surprises, the principal was on it. It was a beautiful, shiny bicycle.

And now the people really cheered. Mama and Papa joined Benjy at the front of the room. There were tears in Benjy's eyes.

"Don't cry," Mama said.

"They are glad tears, Mama," Benjy said. "They keep squeezing out."

When everyone had quieted down, an old man with a crooked cane came slowly up the aisle to the front of the room.

"It is Ogre Magee," the children whispered. "What is he going to do?"

Mr. Magee held up his hand for everyone to be quiet.

"I am a very old man," he said. "I have no children and I have no wife. I am all alone in this world, and I have been a selfish old man. A selfish old man on a beautiful farm. It has taken a little boy to show me that there are beautiful things at Lake Magee which my eyes have never really seen. And so, tonight, I want to invite you to have your summer school picnic at Lake Magee. Also, when I am no longer here my farm will belong to the school for all the picnics in all the years to come."

Mama stepped close to him. She took his hand.

"Poems are pretty talk," she said, "but what you just said was the prettiest talk I ever heard."